ICE CREAM SOUP

Adapted by Gail Herman
Based on a story by Jack Kent
Illustrated by R.W. Alley

A Random House PICTUREBACK® READER

Random House 🏠 New York

Text copyright © 1990 by Random House, Inc. Illustrations copyright © 1990 by R.W. Alley. All rights reserved under International and Pan-American Copyright Conventions. Published in the United States by Random House, Inc., New York, and simultaneously in Canada by Random House of Canada Limited, Toronto.

Library of Congress Cataloging-in-Publication Data
Herman, Gail. Ice cream soup / adapted by Gail Herman ; based on a story by Jack Kent ; illustrated by R.W. Alley.
p. cm.–(Random House pictureback reader)   Summary: Sam and Pam take their time bringing home ice cream for the family and find a surprise in the package at the end of their journey. ISBN 0-679-80790-X [1. Ice cream, ices, etc.–Fiction.] I. Kent, Jack. II. Alley, R.W. (Robert W.), ill. III. Title. IV. Series. PZ7.H4315Ic 1990
[E]–dc20 89-43680

Manufactured in the United States of America   1 2 3 4 5 6 7 8 9 10

It is a hot day.

Sam and Pam are going

for ice cream cones.

They go by the new building,
the pizza shop,
the toy shop,
the pet shop.
At last! The ice cream shop!

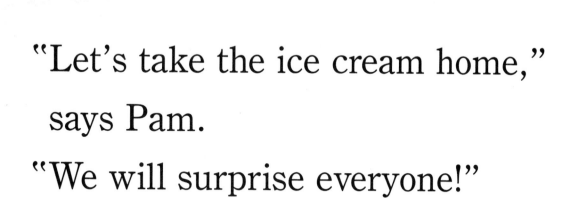

"Let's take the ice cream home,"
says Pam.

"We will surprise everyone!"

"Fudge ripple, please."

Sam and Pam go home.
"Wait! Look at the puppies,"
says Pam.

"Let's go home," says Sam,
"and surprise everyone
with ice cream."

"Wait! Look at the toys,"
says Sam.

"Let's go home," says Pam,
"and surprise everyone
with ice cream."

"Wait! Look at the pizza,"
says Pam.

"Let's go home," says Sam,
"and surprise everyone
with ice cream."

"Wait! Look at the new building," says Sam.

"Let's go home," says Pam,
"and surprise everyone
with ice cream."

At last!

"Look, everyone!" say Pam and Sam.

"We have a surprise!"

It is a surprise.

A surprise for Sam and Pam.

It is not ice cream.

It is ice cream soup.

Yum!

E
Her   Herman, Gail
        Ice cream soup